Worried!

"We'll just have to be patient," Patti advised. "Wait until Stephanie makes up her mind to tell us what's bothering her."

"And you know she can't keep a secret for more than a few hours," said Kate. "I'm sure we'll hear about it this afternoon."

"I hope so," I said. I was getting kind of worried. I'd seen Stephanie get mad before, and I'd definitely seen her sulk before, but I'd never seen her look quite so glum.

As soon as school was over, though, Stephanie rushed out the door.

"Why are you in such a hurry?" Kate asked her, cutting her off at the bike rack.

"I have lots of errands to do," she replied, unlocking her bike. "See you tomorrow." Then Stephanie jumped on her bike and pedaled away.

"She's avoiding us!" Kate said.

"She's avoiding *someone* . . . ," Patti said.

Look for these and other books
in the Sleepover Friends Series:

Stephanie and the Wedding

Susan Saunders

AN
APPLE
PAPERBACK

SCHOLASTIC INC.
New York Toronto London Auckland Sydney

ISBN 0-590-43193-5

12 11 10 9 8 7 6 5 4 3 2 1   0 1 2 3 4 5/9

Printed in the U.S.A.   28

First Scholastic printing, June 1990

Chapter
1

"I can't believe we're actually going to be in a *wedding!*" Stephanie Green exclaimed. "I can just picture the four of us, in gorgeous dresses, carrying armloads of roses and lilies. . . ." She got so caught up in the idea that she closed her eyes for a second and almost steered her bike right into Kate Beekman's.

"Ste-phanie!" Kate yelped, pedaling like crazy to get out of her way. "It was nice of Ms. Chipley to ask us to be junior bridesmaids and everything," she said, once Stephanie had opened her eyes and straightened out her front wheel. "But I can't imagine the same dress looking good on all four of us. Can you, Lauren?"

She was talking to me — I'm Lauren Hunter — and no, I couldn't. Stephanie has black hair and dark eyes, and she's short. Kate is blonde and blue-eyed, and she's shorter and slimmer than Stephanie. I have dark-brown hair and brown eyes, and I'm tall and skinny. And Patti Jenkins has medium-brown hair, green eyes, and pale skin, and she's the tallest girl in fifth grade.

"Do you know what color the dresses will be, Patti?" I asked her, since it was Patti's Uncle Nick who was getting married to Ms. Chipley.

Patti shook her head. "Ms. Chipley — I mean, Tara . . . ," she corrected herself — after all, even though Ms. Chipley *was* our substitute teacher for a while, and you don't exactly call a teacher by her first name, now she was going to be Patti's aunt — "hasn't decided yet."

"What about black?" Stephanie suggested. "*Everybody* looks good in black! And maybe with a little bit of red trim here and there . . ." As you can probably guess, Stephanie's favorite color combination is red and black. That day, for example, she was wearing black jeans, a red shirt, and a red-and-black plaid vest.

"Forget it," I told her. "I look awful in black!

Totally drab. And red washes me out completely."

"I don't think black is a good color for a wedding, anyway," Patti said doubtfully.

"And neither is red!" Kate added. "What about green bridesmaids' dresses?" Green happens to be Kate's favorite color.

"Not green!" I groaned. I have sort of olive skin, and green makes me look like a sick lizard. "How about blue? Stephanie would look great in blue, and you would, too, Kate. And Patti and I . . ."

"Patti?" Kate interrupted me, peering at Patti concernedly.

Patti might have been a million miles away from Riverhurst Main Street. She was pedaling along in a droopy and distracted way, with a faraway expression in her eyes. At last, she felt Kate and Stephanie and me staring at her. "Did you say something?" she asked, giving us kind of a crooked smile.

"Are you OK?" Kate wanted to know.

"Fine," Patti said quickly. But she certainly didn't sound fine.

"You're not upset that the Chipper's going to be your aunt, are you? The kids at school aren't going to hold it against you," I said.

"The Chipper" was the nickname some of the

guys in 5B, our class at Riverhurst Elementary, gave Ms. Chipley when she substituted for our regular teacher, Mrs. Mead. That was because Ms. Chipley was awfully strict in the beginning. She assigned a ton of homework. She also sent lots of people to the principal's office, including Henry Larkin, a boy Patti's kind of interested in.

But Ms. Chipley loosened up after she got to know us all better. And her meeting Uncle Nick, who was staying at Patti's house at the time, didn't hurt either.

"No. It's not that," Patti said as we bumped our bikes up over the curb in front of Gene's Country Meat Market. "It's just such a big change. It was hard when Uncle Nick took the job in Europe. But he's still the same person. He always pays so much attention to Horace and me when he's around." Horace is Patti's little brother. "But I'm afraid that once Uncle Nick's gotten married . . ."

"You won't matter as much to him?" Kate asked.

Patti nodded glumly.

"You're totally wrong!" Stephanie declared firmly. "I read an article in *Teen Topics* that said if you love somebody a lot, the way Nick does Ms.

Chipley, you'll come to love everybody you care about more and more."

"Really?" Patti asked.

"Absolutely. The love kind of multiplies, and flows into all the other people you're close to," said Stephanie. "Besides, you want him to be happy, don't you?"

"Oh, yes!" Patti replied. She's crazy about Uncle Nick.

"Well, Ms. Chipley — Tara — makes him really happy," Stephanie said. "Remember how goofy they acted when they were together?" That was before Uncle Nick had to go back to France — he's a chemical engineer there.

Patti nodded, and so did Kate and I. Uncle Nick and Ms. Chipley had spent practically every free minute together from the day they met. They held hands so much that we began to think their fingers would lock permanently if they didn't watch it. They also beamed at each other constantly, and even giggled a lot.

"I know," Patti said. "It's just that Uncle Nick is a lot younger than my other aunts and uncles, and he's the last to get married. And he's so much fun that he's always seemed more like an older brother than a grown-up.''

I could understand how she felt. Uncle Nick *is* great. He can do all kinds of neat things, like he invented a robot named Oddjob, who can clean the house, plus talk and *dance!* He knows how to blow dynamite soap bubbles. And he also does superior magic tricks. He's cute, too, with wavy, blondish-brown hair, a great curly mustache, and nice twinkly blue-gray eyes behind wire-rimmed glasses. It would be too bad if a really cool person like him turned into another run-of-the-mill relative.

''It'll take some getting used to,'' I said sympathetically.

''Just remember what *Teen Topics* says,'' Stephanie reminded Patti.

''I'll try,'' Patti said.

We leaned our bikes against the lamppost next to the front door of Gene's Country Meat Market and walked into the store. Gene, Jr., who's about my dad's age, was standing beside the cash register. Gene, Sr., *his* dad, was sitting on a stool behind a big glass case full of naked chickens and hamburger meat and lamb chops and — yuck — livers, reading the newspaper.

"One roast, please, Mr. Ottavio," I said. "My mom called about it earlier." Mom went back to work full-time this year, and my brother, Roger, and I help out by doing chores after school — stuff like vacuuming downstairs, or washing clothes, or getting dinner ready, which is what I was supposed to do that Friday.

"One roast, coming up," said Mr. Ottavio, Sr. He opened the huge steel refrigerator and pulled out what looked like around a hundred pounds of meat. While he went into action with a long knife and a cleaver, Stephanie burbled, "Anyway, it's so romantic! Uncle Nick comes back to the United States to get engaged to his girlfriend Maureen and gets his heart broken. And then when he's staying with you and Horace while your parents are away, he has to go to a parent-teacher conference with the Chipper — Ms. Chipley — and it's love at first sight!"

Kate sighed. "If only the wedding were some time in the next two weeks, instead of two months from now!" she said. "A wedding is definitely a *milestone!*"

Kate's in the Video Club at school, and the kids were taking turns filming "milestones," important events that happen in everyone's life, like a little kid's first day at school, or getting married, or having a baby.

"In fact, everything's at the wrong time," Kate grumbled. "Your mom had the twins months ago, Stephanie. We're way too late for anybody's first day of school. The wedding's too far away . . . and I'm stuck!"

"What about somebody's first date?" Stephanie said, grinning at Patti and giving her a friendly poke with her elbow. "Like Patti and Hen-ry Lar-kin."

Patti blushed. "My mom won't let me have a date until I'm in high school!" she mumbled. But the mention of Henry seemed to kind of cheer her up.

"Maybe we could try for a comedy video," Kate said slyly. "Lauren and Wayne Miller!"

"Very funny!" I growled, slugging Kate on the arm. Wayne Miller is the grossest boy at Riverhurst Elementary. He's constantly making fun of girls, and his idea of being cool is swallowing lots of air and burping for hours. And, just my luck, he's decided he *likes me!*

Wayne rides by my house at least once a day on his bike. He even hangs around the mall on Saturdays, waiting for us to show up. I've never been so embarrassed about anything in my life, and I've had plenty of embarrassing moments. . . .

Like the time in first grade when Kate and I put on our best dresses and went to Jenny Carlin's birthday party, and sat down right on the cake!

Or the night we accidentally locked ourselves out of Kate's house and tried to climb back in through the basement window, and Mrs. Beekman called the police. Third-grade criminals!

Or the morning Kate and I had to ride home from Stephanie's house with purple gel in our hair, because there was no hot water to wash it out. We looked like freaks, and Donald Foster, the most conceited boy in seventh grade, was standing on his front lawn and saw us! Total bummer!

Of course, all of these were also some of Kate's most embarrassing moments. Maybe I could share Wayne Miller with her, too. . . .

Kate and I have been friends since we were in *diapers*. We're practically next-door neighbors on Pine Street — there's just one house between us. We started playing together when we were babies. By kindergarten, we were best friends. That's when the sleepovers started. Every Friday night, either Kate would sleep over at my house, or I would sleep over at hers. It got to be such a regular thing that Kate's dad named us the Sleepover Twins.

Not that there's anything very twinlike about us. Kate and I don't *act* any more alike than we *look* alike. She's sensible, I have a runaway imagination. She's super-neat, I was *born* messy. I'm kind of a jock, while Kate's idea of exercise is turning on the VCR. Still, we spent thousands of hours together and never had a real argument.

At our sleepovers, we graduated from games of Let's Pretend to Mad Libs and Truth or Dare. Our cooking improved, too. We started out with ice-cube trays full of cherry Kool-Pops, and s'mores melting in the toaster oven. But gradually we worked our way up to Kate's fabulous fudge and my special onion-soup-sour-cream-olives-and-bacon-bits dip, which is yummy with everything from blue-corn chips to Chee-tos. And in all that time, Kate and I never had a major disagreement . . .

. . . until Stephanie Green moved to the other end of Pine Street from the city last year. Stephanie and I got to be friends because we were both in Mr. Civello's fourth-grade class.

Stephanie was fun. She told neat stories about her life back in the city, and she knew tons about clothes and fashion. How many other fourth-graders had already worked out their own style of dressing, like always wearing red, black, and white? I thought Stephanie was great, and I was sure Kate would think so, too. So I asked Stephanie to a sleepover at my house.

Major mistake! Kate was certain that Stephanie was a total airhead who was only interested in shopping, and Stephanie was convinced that Kate was a stuffy know-it-all. The only thing they both agreed on was that neither of them wanted to see the other again. *Ever!*

I'm usually pretty easygoing. But I can be plenty stubborn if I have to be! I wasn't going to give up so quickly. Since all three of us live on Pine Street, I arranged it so that we just naturally fell into the habit of riding our bikes to school at the same time. Then I accidentally-on-purpose made sure Kate and I bumped into Stephanie at the mall a few Saturdays in a row. Finally, when Stephanie invited me to spend a Friday night at her house, I said only if Kate could come, too.

At that sleepover we ate a huge platter of Mrs. Green's scrumptious peanut-butter-chocolate-chip cookies. Then we watched three movies in a row on Stephanie's private TV. Perfect planning, since movies are definitely the way to Kate's heart! I knew we were home free when Kate asked Stephanie to the next sleepover at the Beekmans'. It wasn't long before the Sleepover Twins were a threesome.

Not that Kate and Stephanie suddenly agreed about everything. No way! And *I* was always getting caught in the middle. That's just one of the reasons I was glad when Patti Jenkins showed up in Mrs. Mead's fifth-grade class, along with the three of us.

Patti's from the city, too, although she's as quiet and shy as Stephanie is outgoing. She's just about the smartest kid at Riverhurst Elementary, and one of the nicest. Plus she's even taller than I am!

When Stephanie wanted Patti to be part of our gang, Kate and I both said yes right away. So school had barely started this year, and suddenly there were *four* Sleepover Friends! We do practically everything together, which was why Ms. Chipley had asked all of us to be in her wedding.

"One five-pound chuck roast," Mr. Ottavio, Sr., said, thumping it down on top of the counter, wrapped in brown paper and tied neatly with string. "For you, little lady, that'll be eleven eighty-five."

I counted out the money Mom had given me. Mr. Ottavio, Sr., slipped the roast into a brown shopping bag, and we headed out the door.

Chapter 2

As the four of us pedaled back up West Main Street, Stephanie said dreamily, "I see us in dresses in navy-blue satin . . . or very dark green . . . ballerina length, with satin roses at the waists, held on with small rhinestone clips. Doesn't that sound *perfect?*"

"Stephanie, get a grip on yourself," Kate said. "It's not *your* wedding."

"Ms. Chipley would probably welcome suggestions," Stephanie said huffily. "Right, Patti?"

"Ummm-mmm. I don't know. I guess so," Patti replied cautiously.

We turned left on Hillcrest and whizzed past Riverhurst Elementary. "What's *her* dress going to be like?" Stephanie went on. "Full-length, right, with a long veil?"

"Well, Mom wants her to wear my great-grandmother's dress," Patti said. "Mom wore it to *her* wedding, and she'd like to pass it on to Tara. But Tara's mom's talking about *her* mother's dress."

"She should definitely pick the older one," Stephanie said positively. "What could be cooler than getting married in a real antique wedding dress? You know: 'Something old, something new'? What about her bouquet? Roses and baby's breath, or maybe lilies? And are we having bouquets to match?"

"Stephanie, this is where we turn," I pointed out, braking at Pine Street. Patti lives further up Hill-crest, on Mill Road. "Eight o'clock?" I said to Patti. I was having the sleepover that Friday.

Patti nodded absentmindedly. "Yeah, sure. See you later. 'Bye."

"Do you think she seemed a little more cheerful?" Kate asked, once Patti had ridden away.

"She'll be okay," Stephanie said breezily. "Uncle Nick and Tara make such a great-looking couple, don't they?"

Ms. Chipley is small and pretty, with reddish-brown hair, which she usually wears in a French braid, green eyes, and a cute nose that turns up at the end.

"Tara?" Kate said, raising her eyebrow.

But Stephanie was on a roll. "I know! I'll buy a copy of *Today's Bride* for the sleepover tonight. That way we can get some ideas. . . ." The three of us stopped our bikes on the sidewalk in front of Kate's house, but there was no stopping Stephanie's mouth. "Then I'll do some sketches of us in different dress styles, and Patti can show them to . . ."

"I've got to stick this roast in the oven," I cut in, because Stephanie was talking a-mile-a-minute and I wasn't sure I'd ever get away.

"See you tonight," Kate and Stephanie both said.

I rode past Kate's house and the Fosters', coasted down my driveway, and parked my bike inside the garage. Then I pulled the shopping bag with the roast in it off my handlebars and headed for the back gate.

The second I'd flipped the latch, I realized I'd made a big mistake. But it was too late. . . . Bullwinkle had already hurled himself against the other side of the gate, practically knocking me flat, and burst through it to *freedom!*

Bullwinkle is our dog — Roger's dog, really, since Roger picked him out at the pound when Bullwinkle was just a tiny puppy. The people there said he was mostly cocker spaniel, but he turned out to be mostly Newfoundland. He's coal black, weighs about a hundred and thirty pounds, and when he stands up on his hind legs, he's over five feet tall! When Bullwinkle's really excited, he can absolutely wreck a room in under thirty seconds, which is why he was locked outside that day. I could hear Roger vacuuming in the living room, and the vacuum cleaner drives Bullwinkle totally crazy!

"Hey, Bullwinkle, come here. I've got your *yellow ball!*" I called craftily as he frisked around me, whacking me with his tail. It wasn't true, of course, but Bullwinkle's ball is the only thing that will lure him into the yard once he's escaped. I stretched my arm way back, pretending I was just about to pitch a ball at our back steps. Unfortunately, the shopping bag from Mr. Ottavio's, which I'd hung on my wrist, swung back, too.

Bullwinkle's shiny little black eyes flicked from the hand holding the pretend ball to the dangling bag. *R-r-rippp!* Before I knew it he grabbed the middle of the bag in his teeth, jerked it off my wrist —

and went galloping down the driveway with it!

"Kate! Stephanie! Help!" I yelled, racing after Bullwinkle, and dinner. "Cut him off!"

Stephanie and Kate dropped their bikes and came tearing up the sidewalk toward us. But as soon as Bullwinkle spotted them, he changed direction. He veered off through the Kennans' yard — they just moved in on the other side of my house — and dashed across the street.

"We have to catch him!" I shouted to Kate and Stephanie. "If he scarfs down that roast, Mom will kill me!"

"I will, too," Stephanie puffed as we raced across the street after Bullwinkle. "I was looking forward to leftovers tonight!"

With Mr. Ottavio's bag dangling from his mouth, Bullwinkle gallumphed through the Martins' flower beds, smack into the Baileys' new fence. That stopped him for a second. I watched his big, thick head swing left and right as he plotted his next move.

"Hurry! Maybe we can trap him against the fence!" Kate gasped as we charged up the sidewalk toward him.

But Bullwinkle was too quick for us. He whirled to the left and took off.

"Oh, no!" Kate said, slowing down. "He's gone into old Mr. Winkler's yard!"

Roger calls Mr. Winkler the Scourge of Pine Street. He's the crankiest person in the neighborhood, maybe even in all of Riverhurst. He doesn't like animals, he doesn't like music, he doesn't like kids. Basically, he doesn't like *anything!*

"We can't go in there," Stephanie hissed.

"But I can't just let Bullwinkle eat twelve dollars' worth of meat," I moaned. "Look! He's sitting down."

Bullwinkle had flopped down on Mr. Winkler's stoop and stuck his head into the shopping bag to sniff loudly at his prize.

"Let's grab him while his head's in the bag!" I said.

"No way!" said Stephanie. She was probably remembering that time a few months ago when Mr. Winkler stormed all the way across the street to yell at us for practicing a new dance step to the latest Heat cassette in Kate's driveway.

"We'll be really quiet," I said in a low voice. "Mr. Winkler won't even know we're there. Ple-e-ease?"

"Okay." Kate took charge. "No noise, no talk-

19

ing, no *nothing!* We grab the bag, and the dog, and run for it!"

"Excellent!" I said.

It worked like a charm. Bullwinkle was too caught up in the interesting meat smell to pay any attention to us. We walked right up to him. Kate and I both latched onto his collar. Stephanie snatched the bag off his head. Then, while Kate and I pulled, Stephanie got behind Bullwinkle and pushed. The whole time we didn't make a sound. We'd eased him off the steps and onto the lawn, when all of a sudden the door of the house flew open behind us!

"Just what in the dickens is going on out here?!" Mr. Winkler thundered. For a skinny little man, he has a very loud voice, the kind that makes you jump every time!

"S-sorry, Mr. Winkler," I stammered. "We were — uh — just taking Bullwinkle for a walk."

"Through my yard?!" Mr. Winkler snorted.

"We were just leaving," Kate told him.

Mr. Winkler wagged his bony finger at us. "None too soon! If I ever catch you with that beast on my property again, I'm calling the Animal Control Board!" Then he slammed his door so hard that his front windows rattled.

"The guy must have early-warning radar!" I murmured. "We were totally quiet!"

"He is such an old crab!" Kate said crossly. "What's *his* problem?"

"Maybe he's lonesome," Stephanie suggested as we pulled and pushed Bullwinkle toward home. "Was there ever a Mrs. Winkler?" Her mind was still fixed on romance.

"Who could stand being married to *him?*" Kate asked. I couldn't have agreed more.

We shoved Bullwinkle up my driveway, and edged him through the back gate. Then I banged it shut, and we leaned against it, huffing and panting.

"Thanks, guys," I said when I'd caught my breath.

I took the roast from Stephanie and looked it over. Mr. Ottavio, Sr., had done such a good job wrapping it up that all Bullwinkle had managed to do was break a couple of strings.

"Just make sure there's a big, fat sandwich on rye bread, with plenty of Russian dressing, with my name on it, tonight," Stephanie said. "I must have lost three pounds, *at least,* in the last ten minutes."

Then Stephanie and Kate went home and I stuck the roast in a pan in the oven, along with onions, potatoes, carrots, and tomato juice. Yummm! Pot roast, instead of doggy-dinner!

I just hoped we'd heard the last of Mr. Winkler for the evening. What if he decided to call my parents and complain? I doubted I'd get in much trouble, but still . . .

Chapter
3

Luckily Mr. Winkler didn't call. And the pot roast was excellent. Even my brother Roger, who never raves about anything I do, said so. Best of all, there was plenty left over for sleepover sandwiches. The gang brought over other snacks, too. Patti had made a bowl of her Alaska dip — tuna and cream cheese and other good stuff — and Kate brought a container of her famous super-fudge. The three of us were in the kitchen, loading the food onto two big trays, when Stephanie arrived with the thirtieth-anniversary issue of *Today's Bride*.

"Everything you ever wanted to know about weddings is in here," Stephanie said, slapping the magazine importantly. "For example, did you have any idea that we're supposed to help Ms. Chipley address her wedding invitations?"

Not a *good* idea, considering the way *my* handwriting looks. And Stephanie's isn't much better.

"And we should phone her a lot," Stephanie went on, "to see if she needs us to run errands for her."

"Well . . . uh . . . I'm not sure she . . ." Patti mumbled, but Stephanie didn't miss a beat. "It's all in here, under 'Attendants: Duties,' " she said. "We're supposed to give a bridal shower for her, too. Won't that be fabulous? We can have it at my apartment!"

What Stephanie calls her apartment is this little house her dad built for her in the Greens' backyard so that she'd have some privacy with her new baby brother and sister around. It has sofa beds, a couple of chairs, a stove, a sink, and a tiny bathroom. We've spent a lot of our sleepovers out there, and it's great. But were we equipped to have a bridal shower?

"Are you sure we should have a party for Ms. Chipley?" I asked nervously. "Aren't we a little young? I mean, I don't even know what grown-ups *do* at parties."

"Yeah. Who would we invite? The other girls in 5B?" Kate snickered, reaching into the fridge for a cold can of Dr Pepper. "Besides, doesn't Ms. Chipley have a maid of honor?"

"Her best friend, Amanda Tilton, from Dannerville," Patti said. Dannerville's the next town over. "She's a teacher, too."

"Then I'm sure Amanda will take care of the bridal shower," Kate said to Stephanie.

"Welllll . . . I guess." Stephanie looked a little disappointed that she wouldn't be hostessing a party. Then she brightened up again: "We *do* have to find a really nice present for her, though. I think we should start looking around the mall tomorrow."

"Can we afford anything 'really nice'?" I asked. "When my Aunt Beth got married, one puny silver fork cost fifty dollars!" I didn't want to blow half a year's allowance on a soupspoon!

"We don't have to give silverware or crystal. We can get her sheets, or towels, or even a toaster," Stephanie said. "It's all in here." She waved the magazine. " 'The Forty Most Wanted Items on Any Bride's Gift List.' Lamps, planters, salad bowls, trash cans . . ."

25

"Trash cans don't seem very elegant," Kate said.

"Or romantic . . . ," I added.

"If we stop by my house first, maybe Tara will give us a hint," Patti suggested. "She's coming over to discuss the wedding plans with Mom in the morning."

"Terrific!" said Stephanie. "We can look at pictures of bridesmaids' dresses tonight and show her the ones we like when we see her!"

Kate rolled her eyes at Patti and me, meaning, *Is there no stopping this girl?!* Then Patti suddenly remembered something. "Oh, Kate, I may have a milestone for you. Horace is losing his first tooth!" Horace is six, which is just about the right age for losing front teeth.

"I don't know," Kate said slowly. "I mean, a video of Horace wiggling his front tooth with his tongue wouldn't exactly be thrilling. But maybe if I make up a little scene starring the Tooth Fairy . . ." She frowned, trying to work it out in her head. Then she smiled at Patti. "Thanks. It's definitely better than nothing."

I filled four glasses with ice, stacked four deluxe-sized pot-roast sandwiches with Russian dressing on a plate, and added them to Kate's tray. Patti and

26

Stephanie grabbed spoons and forks and napkins, and we were ready to hole up in my room for the evening.

"Where's Bullwinkle?" Stephanie asked, keeping a wary eye on the sandwiches as I pushed open the kitchen door.

"Locked in the den," I told her, and we headed upstairs.

As soon as the four of us had flopped down on my bedroom floor with the snacks, Stephanie picked up where she'd left off. "This magazine is full of great ideas!" she said. " 'Instead of throwing rice at the wedding, throw birdseed'!"

Kate and Patti and I started to giggle.

"It's two *people* getting married, not two *p-parakeets!*" I chuckled.

"I'm sure Ms. Chipley and Uncle Nick would just love being pelted with cracked corn and sunflower seeds!" Kate added.

Stephanie made a face at us. "This is serious, guys. Don't we want everything to be perfect for them?"

Of course we did. So we all settled down and started leafing through *Today's Bride*. And we did find some really nice dresses. Patti and I liked a dark-blue one with capped sleeves, a velvet top, and a three-quarter-length satin skirt. Stephanie chose a dark-green one, with a pattern of swirly flowers on the train. Kate finally picked out a long dress in dusty pink, with lace at the neck and sleeves, and a matching lace wreath, which the rest of us thought we could live with, too.

"No prices?" I asked, scanning the pages for dollar signs.

Stephanie-the-shopping-expert shook her head. "You have to go to a store that carries these clothes." She turned to the back of the magazine. "Page 105 . . . San Francisco . . . New York . . . Seattle . . . hmmm . . . here's a place in the city that has the pink dress, and it's near Nana's apartment!" Nana is Stephanie's grandmother, Mrs. Bricker. "She could pick one up and bring it out with her on Monday for us to look at. She's going to be visiting for a few days."

"*If* Ms. Chipley likes the dress . . . ," Kate cautioned.

"Right. If Ms. Chipley likes it," Stephanie repeated in a distant voice. I could tell she was already imagining how she'd look on the big day.

While we munched on our snacks we flipped through the magazine one more time to make sure we hadn't missed anything. Then Kate switched on my parents' portable TV, which we always borrow for sleepovers. "Hey," she said excitedly, "*Friday Chillers* is showing *Bride of Frankenstein*! The old black-and-white version!"

"I love *her* dress!" Stephanie declared enviously, snagging a piece of fudge.

Scary movies don't agree with me. They make my imagination — and my stomach — sit up and jump around. But this one happened to fit in with the wedding theme. So we all watched it, until my parents turned off the lights downstairs and went to bed. Then the movie started to get *really* hairy, and I reached for the remote and switched off the TV set.

"Come on, Lauren," Kate complained. "We were just getting to the good part!"

"No way," I told her. "I'll bet you've seen that movie at least twenty times anyhow!"

"Twelve," Kate replied weakly. Like I said, she's a movie *freak!*

"Besides, we haven't played Truth or Dare in a while," I added.

Chapter
4

I guess Kate had let her guard down for a moment, or maybe she was too full of snacks to risk a dare that might mean a lot of racing around. "Truth," she said, lolling back lazily.

"Excellent! Heh, heh, heh." I rubbed my hands together and grinned wickedly at her. "Who . . ."

"Oh, no!" Kate groaned. "I know what's coming!"

"Who do you *like* now?" Stephanie and I both said it at the same time.

Ever since Kate announced that she wasn't interested in Royce Mason anymore — he's a seventh-grader whose sister, Sally, is in our class — we'd been trying to get her to tell us who she *does* like.

31

And each time she's managed to wriggle out of answering somehow. But not this time!

"Can I switch it to 'dare,' Lauren?" Kate pleaded. "Pretty please. . . ."

"Uh-uh." I stood firm.

"You know how the game works, Kate," Stephanie said briskly. "You chose 'truth,' and now you're going to have to spill the beans or declare *forfeit!*"

"All right, ALL RIGHT!" Kate grumbled. "Tay-*mumble Mumble.*"

Stephanie and Patti and I leaned closer, but she lowered her voice so much that all we could make out was the beginning of the first word.

"What?" Patti asked.

"Who?" I pressed her.

"Speak up!" said Stephanie.

"TAYLOR SPROUSE!" Kate practically screeched.

You could have knocked Patti, Stephanie, and me over with a feather!

"Taylor Sprouse?!" I shrieked. " 'The fathead whose favorite topic is himself'?"

" 'That no-talent rock-and-roller'?" Stephanie said.

" 'Is he the worst, or what?' " Patti added.

All of which were exact quotes from the mouth of Kate Beekman herself on the subject of *Taylor Sprouse!* Had she ever changed her tune!

Taylor Sprouse is a sixth-grader. He does happen to be good-looking, but he ruins it by acting like he's Mr. Super-Cool of the universe and like everyone else in the world — except for a handful of his sixth-grader friends — is a total dork. He dresses all in black. Black sweatshirt, black jeans with a hole in one knee, black high-top sneakers. He also plays really bad electric guitar, and hardly ever bothers to talk to anyone except to say stuff like "Wow," or "Really radical, dude!" And the last *we* heard, Kate couldn't stand him!

"Do you have a secret life we don't know about?" Stephanie demanded.

"Yeah," I said. "Are you the real Kate Beekman or an alien imposter?"

"I've gotten to know Taylor better since he joined the Video Club," Kate said crossly. "And he happens to be *good!* He did this great video about his little cousin's turtle dying that made everybody cry, including Ms. Gilberto!" She's the Video Club sponsor.

"Taylor Sprouse?" I began. "I mean, his *music*

is so awful that you want to cry, but . . ." Kate glared at me and shut me up.

"Now you know why I didn't want to tell you guys," Kate muttered.

"And is that why this 'milestones' thing is so important?" Stephanie said shrewdly.

"I *always* try to do a good job on my videos!" Kate said huffily. After all, she wants to be a great movie director some day. "Patti, truth or dare?"

The game went on pretty calmly for a while. Kate picked Patti, and Patti Stephanie, and Stephanie me, and I picked Patti again. All of us chose "truth." I guess all of us were following Kate's example.

Anyway, we found out that Bobby Krieger had actually *kissed* Stephanie at the school costume party a few weeks before. He also kissed Patti and Jane Sykes and Tracy Osner — Bobby Krieger's just a kissing fool! We also found out the worst grade Patti ever made in her life: a B − in spelling two years ago. But it didn't really count because she had a 102 degree fever and didn't realize it.

Then Patti picked Kate, and asked her something easy. "Who was the first boy you ever liked?"

I already knew the answer to that one: David Lucas. He was a friend of my brother's, tall, thin, with dark hair, and he was always taking pictures. I think maybe it was his *camera* that Kate really liked, so things haven't changed all that much. Kate was six, and David was twelve, and he didn't know she was alive. Then his family moved to Illinois, and that was the end of that.

Now it was Kate's turn to pick somebody. "Lauren," she said, "truth or dare?"

Truths are interesting enough, but I was ready for a little excitement. "Dare," I replied.

And that's when Kate zinged me for pinning her down about Taylor Sprouse. "Great!" she said, staring at me coolly. "Go outside . . . cross the street . . . and knock on Mr. Winkler's front door!"

"You're kidding!" I was stunned. Okay, we weren't supposed to go outside at all after my parents have gone to bed, but I have to admit that we've done it plenty of times, usually playing Truth or Dare. But crossing the street? *And* knocking on Mr. Winkler's door, after the fit he'd had that day? It sounded pretty hair-raising.

"Kate, that's too hard!" Patti said, shocked.

"Lauren did say 'dare,' " Stephanie pointed out, trying not to sound too eager.

"Of course, you could *forfeit*," Kate said, getting

her digs in. "But you know what that means."

We have a long-standing rule that if anyone ever refuses to answer a "truth," or turns down a "dare," that person has to do everything for the girl who picked her for a whole week. That means stuff like carrying her books to school and back, cleaning her room, taking over her chores — you name it! No one has ever forfeited, and I sure wasn't going to be the first.

"Never mind," I said to Patti, frowning at Stephanie and Kate. "I'll do it."

I opened the door to my room as quietly as I could and peered down the hall. My parents' bedroom light was off, so I knew they were already asleep. "All clear!" I whispered, trying to sound braver than I felt. I crept down the stairs, with Kate, Stephanie, and Patti right behind me. When I got to the bottom, I marched straight to the front door.

Suddenly Kate tugged at my sweatshirt. "Lauren," she said in my ear. "You don't really have to do this. I just wanted to shake you up a little, because of Taylor."

"I said 'dare,' " I hissed back snippily, "didn't I?" I unlocked our front door slo-o-owly, so that there was hardly even the smallest click. Then I stuck my head outside.

Pine Street was absolutely still. Even all the neighborhood dogs were fast asleep. And all the windows in all the houses across the street were dark — the Martins', the Baileys', and old Mr. Winkler's.

I stepped onto our front porch and took a couple of deep breaths while I looked around. The closest street lamp is the one in front of the Kennans', next door. It looked awfully bright. I was glad I was wearing dark clothes — my sweatshirt was royal blue, and I had on jeans and dark-gray hightops. As long as I stayed out of the street lamp's circle of light, I should be okay. Unless a car turned up the block. . . .

"What time is it?" I asked.

Patti checked her watch. "Eleven thirty-five."

Roger wouldn't be driving back from his date with Linda for another thirty minutes at least, and Todd Schwartz — he's Stephanie's across-the-street neighbor at the end of the block — usually stays out even later.

I squared my shoulders. "Here I go," I murmured to the silent group huddled behind me.

I dashed down the steps and across my yard, being careful to stay away from the light in front of the Kennans'. I cut across the street and ducked down next to the Baileys' new fence. I sidled along it until I reached the edge of Mr. Winkler's lawn. Then I crouched down, and checked out the enemy territory.

Mr. Winkler's house was pitch-black. Not a glimmer of light was showing, front or back. His yard is plain old grass, with no bushes for me to bump into or flower beds to trip over. All I had to do was sprint up to his door, tap once (Kate didn't say to knock *loud* or *long*) and race back to the Baileys' fence again. Then I'd cut through the Martins' yard — unlike Bullwinkle, I'd spare their flowers — across Pine Street, and straight through my front door.

"Piece of cake, Lauren," I said to psych myself up. But somehow I didn't really believe it.

Still, a dare's a dare. So I shot up like a spring, raced full speed across Mr. Winkler's perfect grass, dashed up his steps on my tiptoes, and tapped his door. For a split-second, I imagined him popping out from behind it, like a mean old jack-in-the-box. Then I sped back down his steps, across to the Baileys' and then the Martins', before I absolutely flew back across the street. Kate was holding the door open for me, her eyes wide.

"Safe!" I gasped, collapsing on the floor in the hall. I don't think I'd breathed more than once since I'd left my front porch!

"Lauren," Kate hissed. "He saw you!"

"Cut it out!" I said crossly. "It was scary enough. . . ."

"No, she's right. He *must* have!" Patti said. "Because just a couple of seconds after you knocked — "

"His porch light flicked on!" Stephanie ended Patti's sentence for her.

I scrambled to my feet and squinted through the glass pane in our front door. My hair practically stood on end, like the lady in *Bride of Frankenstein*. They *weren't* teasing! Mr. Winkler's porch light was on!

"Radar!" I mumbled breathlessly. I felt like hiding. Knowing Mr. Winkler, turning on a light to frighten me out of my wits was just the beginning! What would his next move be?

I didn't have to wonder long. When the telephone rang, I had a pretty good idea who it was! We dashed into the kitchen and stood paralyzed, staring at the wall phone, as it finished its first ring and started on its second.

"I'm done for!" I moaned. "No need to get *me* a dress for Uncle Nick's wedding. I'll be grounded! I'll probably still be grounded at my *own* wedding! . . ."

Kate grabbed the phone as the third ring began. "Hello?" she said in a low, sleepy voice. She actually sounded quite a lot like my mom.

"Mrs. Hunter? Mrs. Hunter, I think you should know that your daughter is wandering the neighborhood in the middle of the night, up to no good!" Kate had turned the receiver so that we could all hear Mr. Winkler, but he was yelling so loud we could probably have heard him *without* the phone!

"I'm so sorry — " Kate began in her "mom" voice.

But Mr. Winkler wasn't having any of it. "That's all very well, Mrs. Hunter. But I think this has gone far enough. First it was that drooling hound" — poor Bullwinkle! — "and now your badly behaved child!" *Child?!* I beg your pardon! "This absolutely must not continue, or I'll have to take *steps!*" And with that he slammed his phone down.

Kate hung ours up without a word. The four of us were practically rooted to the floor!

Then Bullwinkle started to bark — the den is right next to the kitchen.

"Lauren, is everything okay down there?" my mom called down the stairs. "Was that the telephone?"

"Wrong number, Mrs. Hunter," Stephanie managed to call back.

" 'Night, Mom," I said. "And thanks, Kate," I added in a murmur.

But I was ninety-nine percent sure we hadn't heard the last of the dreaded Mr. Winkler.

Chapter
5

The four of us had breakfast in a hurry the next morning — scrambled eggs, sausages, and blueberry muffins. I was so worried that Mr. Winkler would decide he had something further to say to my mom about my midnight visit that I practically ate with my fingers crossed.

"That guy has to get out and do things," Stephanie murmured, taking a big bite of muffin. "What he needs is a friend! What about Mrs. Carter?"

"Mrs. Carter?" Patti said. "Stephanie, she must be at least twenty years older than he is!" Mrs. Carter lives a couple of blocks over, and she used to teach my *mom* in elementary school!

"Plus Mrs. Carter is almost as crotchety as Mr.

Winkler," I pointed out, spearing another sausage. "*Not* a good combination."

"Stephanie, don't tell me you're trying to fix up Mr. Winkler?" Kate giggled. "I think Uncle Nick's wedding has gone to your brain!"

"A social life never hurt anyone!" Stephanie replied indignantly. "Maybe we should make a list of names . . ."

But I just wanted to get as far away from Mr. Winkler as possible!

As soon as we'd finished eating, and Kate had run home for her club's video camera, Roger gave us all a ride to Patti's. Ms. Chipley's blue car was already parked in the Jenkinses' driveway when we got there, and Horace was outside, squirting something with the hose.

"Artificial respiration for a turtle?" Stephanie asked Patti. Horace keeps a whole collection of creepy-crawlies — turtles, lizards, even a snake or two — in the basement.

As we started up the walk, Kate held the camera up to her eye. "Horace?" she called. "How's the tooth doing?" She pressed down the "on" switch, and the camera started to whir.

Horace looks a lot like Patti, only he's bonier

43

and his ears stick out a little. He's also a kid of few words. "Gone," he said. Then he grinned, and I could see the gap in the front of his mouth from twenty feet away.

"Nuts!" said Kate, taking her finger off the switch. "Another 'milestone,' down the tubes."

"When did that happen?" Patti asked her brother.

"Last night," Horace answered. "I was eating a Popsicle."

"What are you washing?" Stephanie wanted to know. Horace's jeans and sneakers were streaked with dirt, and he had the hose aimed at what looked like four or five mud pies lined up at the bottom of the steps.

"Artifacts," Horace answered briefly.

Artifacts?! I'd never even *heard* the word! On the other hand, *I'*m not a six-year-old genius.

Kate raised an eyebrow curiously at Patti — I guess she'd never heard it, either.

"He picked the word up from Mom," Patti explained apologetically. Patti's mother's a professor of ancient history at the university. "Artifacts are really old things, like the stuff people find buried in tombs in Egypt."

"So where were *these* artifacts buried?" Kate asked Horace. Under the stream of water from the hose, one of the larger mud pies proved to be a wrinkled brown shoe.

"They're digging up the old water pipes on Halsey Lane, and putting in new ones," Patti said. Halsey's the next street off Hillcrest after Patti's street, Mill Road. "Horace goes there and sifts through the dirt for buried treasure."

"Find anything good?" I asked him as he directed the water *into* the shoe. It was a woman's high-heel, sort of thick at the bottom.

"A real silver buckle," Horace said proudly.

"A rusty belt buckle," Patti whispered.

"And a big diamond pin," Horace added.

"A rhinestone earring," said his sister under her breath.

Horace put the hose down, turned the shoe over, and shook it hard. A little ball of mud fell out on the steps with a clunk.

"Sounds like a rock," said Stephanie, poking it with her finger. "Hmmmm. . . ." She picked up the mud ball and stuck it in front of the water from the hose for a minute. "Look!" she exclaimed. "It's a ring!"

Stephanie held it up so that Patti, Kate, and I could see it, too. It was gold-colored, with a green stone in the center, and there was lettering on the sides.

Kate took the ring and rubbed off more of the mud. "Riverhurst High School!" she read. "It's a senior ring from *1942!* It's almost fifty years old!"

"Wow! I wonder how it ended up stuck in that shoe," I said.

"I wonder who it belonged to!" Stephanie said.

"Senior rings usually have initials inside them, don't they?" asked Patti.

"That's right!" Kate agreed, squinting at the band. "It's still too dirty to make them out, though."

"Let's take it into the house and wash it with soap," Patti suggested, starting up the steps.

"Hey!" Horace called after us crossly. "That's *my* treasure. Give it back!"

"If you let us have it, I'll buy you another lizard at Feathers and Fins," Patti said.

"Deal," said Horace, pointing the hose at the next mud blob.

We'd gotten so involved with the ring that we'd sort of forgotten about Ms. Chipley. But as we went into the house we spotted her sitting in the dining room with Mrs. Jenkins. Both of them were absolutely surrounded with scraps of paper.

"I've got the names of over a hundred people that Nick *has* to invite, added to your eighty-seven," Mrs. Jenkins was saying.

"Two hundred people?" Ms. Chipley exclaimed. She sounded sort of overcome by the thought.

Actually, she didn't look like she was having much more fun thinking about the wedding than Patti had been. So who was? Besides Stephanie, of course, although Stephanie couldn't really be considered a member of the family . . .

Patti's mom, for one. "Two hundred at the very least!" she repeated with satisfaction. "A nice, big ceremony, and a lovely reception at the Pequontic Inn afterward. The inn is right on the river, and it's just lovely at this time of year!

"Of course we'll have to have a bride's table for the bridal party, the parents' table, the toast to the bride and groom, flowers . . ." Mrs. Jenkins was scribbling in a little notebook as she talked. Then she put her pen down, glanced up, and saw us in the hall. "Good morning, girls. We're just making arrangements for the wedding!"

Ms. Chipley said hi, too, but her eyes kept straying uneasily to the pieces of paper around her.

Then Stephanie added another paper to the pile. She pulled the page with the dusty-pink floor-length dress on it out of her pocket and unfolded it. "We looked through *Today's Bride*," she explained, "and we wondered how you'd like us in this dress."

"Very pretty," Ms. Chipley mumbled sort of absently. "Amanda Tilton, my maid of honor, likes pink, too. I'll show this to her."

"Fabulous!" said Stephanie. "I'll call Nana tonight and ask her to bring one out from the city when she comes, so we can try it on!"

"Ms. Chipley, could you give us a hint for a wedding present?" Kate said.

For the first time that morning, Ms. Chipley really *looked* at us. "That's very sweet of you," she replied warmly, "but it certainly isn't necessary. As soon as Nick and I announced our engagement, we were flooded with gifts."

"But it's one of the attendants' duties!" Stephanie said. "We *have* to get you a present."

"Oh. In that case . . ." Ms. Chipley thought for a second. "How about a big bath towel?"

Today's Bride was right! And even a super-deluxe bath towel only costs ten or fifteen dollars, as opposed to *fifty*. The four of us could handle that with no problem.

"What color?" I asked her.

"I think . . . dark-green would be nice," Ms. Chipley replied, and Kate nodded approvingly.

"Duck à l'orange for the main course?" Mrs. Jenkins murmured to herself. "Or the Chicken Supreme?" As Mrs. Jenkins went back to the wedding plans, Ms. Chipley's face set in a worried frown.

But the four of us raced upstairs to the bathroom sink. After Kate had attacked the ring with lots of soap and a nailbrush, we dried it off and held it under Patti's desk lamp.

The initials were tiny, and very faint, but Patti managed to read them. "A . . . L . . . D. Alan? Alex?" she guessed.

"It's a girl's ring," Kate corrected her.

"Just because it was stuck in a lady's shoe?" I asked.

"Nope," Kate said. "Boys' rings are a lot bigger and heavier. My dad's college ring weighs a ton."

Patti slipped the ring on her finger. It was loose, but not enormous. "I wonder who she was."

"Is. She's probably still alive," Kate said.

"Yeah. She'd only be in her" — I added in my head — "middle sixties by now."

"Nana's age. Hey, maybe Dad has some clients who went to Riverhurst High around that time!" Stephanie said. Mr. Green is a lawyer at Blake, Binder, and Rosten. "I'll ask him about it tonight."

"I'll ask my mom, too," I told her. Mom works at Sawyer Insurance.

But it just so happened that we got a lead before that at Gene's Country Meat Market!

First, though, Mr. Jenkins dropped us off at the mall. To give us strength for wedding present shopping we each had a slice of double-cheese pizza with pepperoni, meatballs, and olives, and a Cherry Coke at the Pizza Palace. Then we window-shopped at Just Juniors. They had a great velvet vest with gold charms sewed all over it that was *to die for!*

Afterward we went to Stan's Home Furnishings and got down to serious business. I never knew there were so many different kinds of dark-green towels in the world! Naturally, Kate and Stephanie insisted that we look carefully at each one, so we didn't come to any agreement that afternoon. But we at least narrowed down our choices to a dark-green herringbone, a dark-green-and-gray striped, or a forest-green with little black and white dots. Then we had to run, because Mrs. Beekman was picking us up at the side door of the mall at three.

Before Kate's mom drove us all home, though, she stopped by Gene's Country Meat Market. And while Gene, Jr., trimmed some lamb chops for Kate's dad to cook for their Saturday dinner — Dr. Beekman is a terrific cook — the four of us checked out the ring again.

"Senior rings really haven't changed much in fifty years," Stephanie was saying, when Gene, Sr., spoke up from behind the cash register.

"What have you got there?" he asked. "Hey, is that an old Riverhurst High ring?"

Kate nodded. "From 1942. Patti's little brother found it, and we'd like to return it to its owner if we can."

"Nineteen forty-two! You don't say!" Mr. Ottavio, Sr., exclaimed, stepping around the counter to take a close look. "I graduated in '44 myself."

"You did? Did you know any of the kids two years ahead of you?" Stephanie asked excitedly.

"Some of them." Mr. Ottavio, Sr., reached for the ring and adjusted his glasses. "Girl's ring, initials A . . . L . . . D. There was Amy, Annette, Alice . . .

but none of those girls had last names that began with D." He rubbed his forehead, concentrating. "Nope. Nothing springs to mind," he said at last, handing the ring back to Patti.

"Tell you what you do," Gene, Jr., said — he'd overheard part of the conversation while he sliced the lamb. "Go to the high school library. They have a whole section of old yearbooks. Find the right year, match up a girl with the initials, and you've got your answer. It's as easy as one, two, three."

"The principal's office may have an address for you, too," Mrs. Beekman added. "Schools usually like to keep track of their graduates."

"The high school library!" said Stephanie. "That'll be fun!"

Chapter
6

Actually, I found the idea of crashing the high school library kind of nerve-wracking. Kids Roger's age always act so superior! Since I'd noticed Mr. Winkler out weeding his lawn anyway, I made myself scarce on Sunday and stayed indoors trying to put together the right outfit for the occasion. . . .

Even so, on Monday morning I changed clothes at least four times. I didn't want to look like a little twerp with all those sixteen-, and seventeen-, and eighteen-year-olds around. On the other hand, I didn't want to look like I was playing "dress-up," either. I finally decided that the important thing was to be comfortable, especially since I was probably going to *feel* uncomfortable. What would Roger say when he saw me at his school, for example? Not a fun subject to think about. So I ended up putting on my maroon-and-white button sweater over a white turtleneck and jeans. Kate wore her short denim skirt, a yellow pullover, and matching tights, Patti her pink-and-green sweats, and Stephanie her red-and-black printed overalls. And as soon as our classes were over at three, we headed toward the high school to test our outfits on the older kids.

Riverhurst Middle School is just down the block from Riverhurst Elementary, and you cut through their football and soccer fields to get to the high school, which is just behind them.

A bunch of middle school boys were kicking a soccer ball around as we walked past, and a stocky guy with curly brown hair yelled, "Hey, Kate!"

It was Royce Mason, the guy Kate used to like.

"He is definitely cute," Stephanie said to Kate.

Kate shrugged. "There are more important things than sports," she said loftily.

The high school doesn't get out until three-thirty, thank goodness, so everybody was still in class when we ran up the wide marble steps and through the main door. Our first stop was the office of the school secretary, Mrs. Dennison.

Stephanie told her about the ring. "We'd like to go to the library and try to find out who it belonged to," she explained.

"Good idea," said Mrs. Dennison. "Just walk to the end of this hall, turn left, then right in the middle of the next corridor. And if you come back here with a name, I may be able to help you out with an address."

So we tiptoed down a couple of long halls, glancing through open doors at high school kids raising their hands to answer questions, or reading, or taking tests. I spotted Todd Schwartz in one classroom. He was passing a note to his girlfriend, Mary Beth Young. Clearly, *some* things are exactly the same in elementary and high school.

Mr. Dooley is the librarian at the high school, and he led us right to the yearbooks. "These run from 1920 up to the present," he told us. "Forty-one, forty-two . . . a-ha! Here it is." Mr. Dooley pulled out a yearbook with a faded navy cover and handed it to Stephanie. "You should be able to find what you're looking for under 'Seniors,' at the front of the book."

It was like one of those movies where lightning strikes, or a clock runs backward, and you're suddenly flashed back to the past. From the outside, the yearbook might have been one of Roger's. But the minute you flipped it open you were in another world! The boys all had on suits with wide lapels, and these funny ties with wild, swirly patterns. And the girls had long, sleek hairstyles and dark lipstick.

There were about sixty students in the graduating class in 1942, but we found our girl right away: "Annabelle Lee Dodson!" Patti read her name. She had blondish-brown hair, a nice smile, and sparkly dark eyes.

"She looks neat!" Stephanie said. "Annabelle," she told the picture, "we've got your ring."

Underneath Annabelle's name was a list of all the things she'd done in high school. "Sophomore Sweetheart, French Club, four years, and Drama Club, three years. I'll bet she was in some plays!" I said. "Let's look for more pictures of her."

We flipped past the juniors and sophomores. "Stop!" Kate squawked.

"Sssh," Stephanie warned as Mr. Dooley frowned in our direction. We *were* in a library, after all.

"There's Mr. Ottavio!" Kate exclaimed in a whisper.

The picture was about the size of a postage

stamp, but Mr. Ottavio, Sr., didn't look all that different as a boy, except that he's totally gray now and he wears glasses sometimes. He still has the same thick hair, parted on the side, and the same friendly grin. Maybe Annabelle hadn't changed much either.

We leafed past "Freshmen," and "Faculty." All the teachers had stern expressions on their faces. Then we slowed down at "Activities and Events." There were photographs of guys playing football — talk about strange uniforms! — and baseball, and girls tumbling, and shooting off bows and arrows in kind of weird-looking gym suits. Finally we got to pictures of the 1942 Drama Club, and our biggest *shock!*

Kate pointed to a photo of a girl in an old-fashioned dress, leaning toward a thin-faced blond boy in a high-collared shirt, as if she were about to give him a kiss. " 'Annabelle Dodson,' " Kate read aloud, " 'one of our most popular actresses, stars in *Seventeen,* with Harvey Winkler —' "

Kate stopped dead.

"Winkler?!" all four of us hissed at once.

"Our Winkler?" Stephanie said. "Let me see that!" She grabbed the yearbook, held it close to her face, and peered at the blurry picture. "It's his nose, all right — long and narrow and *nosy!*"

"And those look like his ears, too — wide, like a radar dish!" I added, squinting over her shoulder.

"Give me that book!" Kate snatched it away from Stephanie and turned to the front again. "Let's look in 'Seniors' — Reston, Rogers, Sager, Taft, Weiss . . . *Winkler!*"

This time the photograph filled practically half the page, and there was no mistaking it for anyone other than our very own old crab, Mr. Winkler of 18 Pine Street! But in this picture, his hair was slicked back, he was wearing a spotted bow-tie, and he was actually smiling, which was new to us!

"Three years in the Latin Club, four years in the Drama Club, he played on the baseball team. . . ." Patti was reading what was printed under his picture.

"And the football team!" I was amazed. Football players must have been a lot smaller in those days. Todd Schwartz is the size of a grizzly bear!

"So he wasn't always such a pill," Stephanie said. She picked up the yearbook and flipped forward to "Activities and Events" again, to the photo of Annabelle and Mr. Winkler. "He sure looks happy enough here," she went on. "I wonder . . ."

The three-thirty bell rang, and the high school

kids came barreling out of their classrooms, like Bull-winkle when he spots an open gate.

"We'd better catch Mrs. Dennison before she leaves, for Annabelle's address," Kate said.

We put the yearbook back on the shelf, thanked Mr. Dooley, and joined the horde of people jamming the halls.

"Excuse us . . . going through . . . sorry . . ." We squeezed around the mob of yakking freshmen, sophomores, juniors, and seniors, and for once I didn't feel like a giant, the way I usually do in *elementary* school!

"Hey, squirt! What're you doing here?" It was Roger, pushing in the opposite direction, on his way to track practice. His best friend, Sam Conti, was with him. "Hello, ladies!" Sam said, and "Looking good, Lauren!" So I guess my outfit was okay for high school, after all.

We yelled good-bye and the crowd swept us along, until we sort of popped out in front of Mrs. Dennison's door.

She found the address for us right away in one of her files. "She's now Annabelle Dodson Brant," Mrs. Dennison told us as she jotted the information down on a slip of paper. "She lives at 27 Columbine

59

Avenue in Dannerville. I'm sure she'll be just thrilled to get her ring back!"

"Thanks very much," Stephanie said, taking the paper and sticking it in her tote.

The mob of high school kids had thinned out a little. We hustled down the marble steps, cut across the middle school playing fields, and headed for our bikes.

"Maybe we should call Annabelle this afternoon, to let her know that we'll be mailing the ring to her," Kate said.

"Are you crazy?!" Stephanie exclaimed. "And miss a once-in-a-lifetime opportunity?"

"What once-in-a-lifetime opportunity?" I asked.

"To turn Mr. Winkler's lonely, humdrum life around!" Stephanie replied. "We'll send a letter to Annabelle Brant with the ring, telling her how finding it really brought back memories of Riverhurst High School, and mention the play, and suggest that maybe she might like to get together and talk over the old days. . . ."

"With *us?*" Patti said, still not understanding.

But I thought *I* was beginning to. It was all more of the if-you-really-like-somebody-you'll-like-everybody-better business that Stephanie had read in *Teen*

Topics. If Mr. Winkler and Annabelle got together, then he would feel more kindly toward all of us. Or something like that!

"Of course not!" Stephanie was saying to Patti. "We're going to sign the letter 'Harvey.' "

"*Harvey?*" Kate said, not ready to believe what she was hearing.

"That's correct," Stephanie said with a grin. "As in Harvey *Winkler!*"

Chapter
7

When we said good-bye to Patti at the corner and turned off onto Pine Street, we were all still arguing about Stephanie's latest brain wave. "It's a really bad idea," Kate insisted. "Annabelle is obviously married, anyway!"

"Maybe she's divorced. Or widowed, like Nana," Stephanie said. "Notice how her name is *Annabelle Dodson Brant,* and not 'Mrs. John R. Brant,' or whatever? That probably means there's no Mr. Brant now."

Kate shook her head. "Stephanie," she groaned, "lots of women go by their own names. Would you want to be known only as Mrs. So-and-So for the rest of your life?"

I was with Kate. Stephanie has come up with some pretty wild plans from time to time, but this one was a prizewinner! "I totally agree," I said as we coasted to a stop at the end of the Beekmans' driveway. "Besides, even if Annabelle isn't married anymore, what if she couldn't *stand* Mr. Winkler in high school?!" That seemed like a strong possibility to me, if his personality then was anything like his personality now!

"Just look over to your right," Stephanie murmured, "but be cool about it!"

To the right were the Martins', the Baileys', and you-know-who's house. So I glanced out of the corner of my eye toward Mr. Winkler's. Sure enough, there he was, scowling at us from his living-room plate-glass window, just waiting for us to mess up!

"If he's this crotchety now," Stephanie went on in a low voice, "how do you think he'll act when we get older, and have big, noisy teenage parties?"

Bummer! And I guess Kate felt the same way, because she suddenly said, "Let's do it. Let's write the letter."

I nodded. "We have nothing to lose," I said.

But Stephanie had to rush home, because Nana would be arriving any minute with the bridesmaid's dress we had picked out. Kate's dad was on duty at the hospital that evening, so she and her mom and Melissa, her little sister, were going to the Burger Joint at the mall. And I had to do two washes before dinner.

We agreed that each of us would compose a letter that night, pretending to be Mr. Winkler, writing to Annabelle Dodson Brant. We'd compare the letters the next day and string together the best parts of each. Then I'd type up the final version on Roger's typewriter and sign it "Harvey Winkler" (we decided that I'd better sign it because I have the crabbiest handwriting). After that we'd mail it with the ring, and see if Mr. Winkler's mood improved in the near future.

Writing isn't my best subject, so mine was short:

Dear Annabelle,
You probably never expected to hear from me after all these years. But I've found something that belongs to you (ring, enclosed), and I wonder if it will remind you of the good old days as much as it does me.
Yours sincerely,
Harvey Winkler

" 'Yours sincerely'?" Kate said the next morning, when we met on the corner of Pine and Hillcrest before school. "Doesn't sound very chummy, does it?"

"What does yours say?" I asked her.

" 'Hoping to hear from you soon,' " Kate replied.

"That sounds like some of the junk mail that we get," I sniffed. "The stuff that starts out, 'To whom it may concern.' "

Patti's just said, "Best," which is how her mother signs notes to professor friends of hers.

Kate shook her head. "I don't think any of these have the right touch. Stephanie's so keen on *love* these days that she's bound to be better at this than we are."

So we were all really looking forward to reading *hers*. "Hey, Stephanie!" I called out as soon as I spotted her pedaling toward us. "How did you sign your Harvey letter?"

But Stephanie didn't stop to show us her version. Instead she just muttered, "We're going to be late," and took off around the corner. Kate shot a baffled look at Patti and me, and Patti shrugged her shoulders, just as puzzled.

The three of us had to pedal hard to catch up with Stephanie on Hillcrest, and she didn't exactly act overly friendly.

"Did Nana come?" Patti asked her.

"Yeah," Stephanie mumbled.

"Did she bring the bridesmaid's dress?" I said.

Stephanie just nodded. What happened to the usual bubbly Stephanie Green? This was like pulling teeth!

"Do you like it?" Kate wanted to know.

"It's okay," Stephanie said shortly. "We'd better hurry. It's almost time for the bell."

We didn't get much more out of her at lunch, either.

"Did you try the dress on?" said Kate in the cafeteria line.

And Stephanie murmured, "Not yet."

Stephanie Green not trying on new clothes immediately?! She didn't eat her barbecued ribs on a bun, either, and barbecued ribs are her favorite school lunch. Either she was sick, or *really* upset about something. And she didn't *look* sick, so . . .

I gave it one more shot. I pushed my tray back, took my Winkler letter out of my jeans, and said,

"It's time to get down to business. Where's yours, Stephanie?"

"I didn't do one," Stephanie muttered. "It was a dumb idea, anyway." She stood up and picked up her tray. "Listen, I didn't finish my social studies homework, so I'm going back to 5B to work on it. See you later."

As we watched Stephanie dumping her lunch in the bin and trudging out the door, Kate said, "There's definitely something happening that we don't know about."

"Since we saw Stephanie yesterday afternoon," Patti agreed. "But what?"

"Here's what we do know: Nana came to Riverhurst from the city. And she brought the bridesmaid's dress with her," I said.

"But Nana would never do anything to upset Stephanie," Patti said. "And even if Stephanie hated the dress, we could always pick out something else."

"So it has to be something really major," Kate said. "Something to do with the twins, maybe?"

"I don't think so," I said. "I mean, she was a little freaked out about them in the beginning, but now she really gets along with Emma and Jeremy."

"We'll just have to be patient," Patti advised. "Wait until Stephanie makes up her mind to tell us what's bothering her."

"And you know she can't keep a secret for more than a few hours," said Kate. "I'm sure we'll hear about it this afternoon."

"I hope so," I said. I was getting kind of worried. I'd seen Stephanie get mad before and I'd definitely seen her sulk before, but I'd never seen her look quite so glum.

As soon as school was over, though, Stephanie rushed out the door.

"Why are you in such a hurry?" Kate asked her, cutting her off at the bike rack.

"I have lots of errands to do," she replied, unlocking her bike. "See you tomorrow." Then Stephanie jumped on her bike and pedaled away, in the opposite direction from Pine Street.

"She's avoiding us!" Kate said.

"She's avoiding someone . . . ," Patti said.

"I told Mom I'd go straight home to wait for the man who's coming to clean our couch," I said then. "You guys want to come with me? We could work on Harvey's letter." At least the rest of us could stick together, and maybe Stephanie would call . . .

"That's okay with me," said Kate.

"Sure," Patti said. "I'll phone my mom from there."

So we biked to my house, made a few peanut-butter-and-banana sandwiches, and poured three glasses of Dr Pepper. Then we got to work at the kitchen table. We borrowed a sentence or two from Kate's letter, and a couple from Patti's and mine. We added some new stuff, too, from one of my mom's books on proper manners. By the time we'd put it all together, I thought the letter sounded just right.

Dear Annabelle,

Enclosed you will find your Riverhurst High School ring, which I was fortunate enough to come across on Halsey Lane, in an excavation. Holding it in my hand brought back so many wonderful memories of our days in the Drama Club, and especially performing in that excellent play, "Seventeen."

If you happen to be passing through Riverhurst in the near future, I would very *much enjoy spending an hour or two with you, reliving some of our good times together.*

My very best wishes,
Harvey Winkler

"It's a little stiff," Kate said, "but I don't think Mr. Winkler could write anything but a stiff letter."

"I think it's perfect!" Patti said.

"Should we send it?" I asked.

Patti nodded. "Remember what Stephanie said? This letter could very well turn Mr. Winkler's lonely life around!"

"If it works, great. And if it doesn't, he'll never find out we're the ones who sent it," Kate pointed out sensibly.

Patti could repeat the address with no problem. She never forgets anything she hears or reads. I'd just started typing the letter — I was using Mom's gray-blue stationery — when Dynamic Furniture Cleaners rang our bell.

Dynamic Cleaning is a noisy process, so we stuck Bullwinkle in the spare room upstairs, and went outside to sit on the front steps. We'd barely started discussing Stephanie again when Patti spoke up. "Hey, isn't that Nana pushing a double stroller up the sidewalk?"

Kate squinted. She's nearsighted, but she only wears her glasses for important movies. "It *is* Nana, with Emma and Jeremy. And . . ."

"*Mr. Kessler?!*" All three of us had recognized the second grown-up at the same time.

We'd met Mr. Kessler when Nana took us with her to the Lost Valley Dude Ranch in Arizona. He lives in Maine, but he was escaping the winter to vacation in the sun, just like we were. He and Nana hung around together most of the time we were in Lost Valley. Mr. Kessler's a nice man, and very handsome, too, with dark, bushy eyebrows and curly steel-gray hair, cut really short.

Kate, Patti, and I rushed down the front steps and out to the sidewalk to meet them. Nana gave each of us a kiss. And Mr. Kessler said, "Remember me?" He gave a big bear hug to the three of us at once.

"Of course we do!" Kate smiled at him. "Are you going to be in Riverhurst long, Mr. Kessler?"

He and Nana exchanged glances. "Didn't

Stephanie tell you?'' Nana asked.

"Tell us what?'' I asked.

"Dan and I are getting married this Saturday,''
Nana said, taking Mr. Kessler's hand. "And we'd like
you all to come to the ceremony.''

Chapter
8

Nana and Mr. Kessler were getting married?! Why hadn't Stephanie said anything about it? Kate, Patti, and I stared at each other, flabbergasted.

"Stephanie just found out herself last night," Nana explained. "She probably hasn't had time to tell you yet."

She only had *all day* at school!

Patti was first to recover. "We'd love to come to your wedding, Mrs. Bricker," she said warmly.

Kate and I nodded, because we were still speechless. "We're Stephanie's best friends!" I was thinking. "Why didn't she tell *us*? Doesn't she want us to be there?" It didn't make any sense!

But Nana was talking again. "The ceremony is

at Judge Frayne's house, at eleven o'clock Saturday morning," she said. "Then we'll have a small reception at home," meaning the Greens'.

"It sounds great!" I'd finally untied my tongue.

"Congratulations!" Kate added.

As soon as Nana and Mr. Kessler and the sleeping twins moved on up the sidewalk, Kate said sternly, "We're calling up Ms. Stephanie Green right now, and getting to the bottom of this!"

Stephanie has her own private number but either she was still out, "doing errands," or she just plain wasn't answering, because she didn't pick up, even though we let it ring and ring. She didn't answer when I called later that evening. Neither did anyone at her parents' number. Maybe they were all out to dinner, celebrating Nana's wedding.

But on Wednesday we cornered her! Patti, Kate, and I all rode to Stephanie's house a little after eight o'clock that morning. We parked ourselves at the bottom of the driveway. There was no way she could give us the slip this time!

While we were waiting, I dropped a little padded envelope with the Winkler letter in it, and Annabelle Dodson Brant's Riverhurst High School ring, into the mailbox. Then I didn't give it another thought. We had more important things to worry about.

Stephanie finally rolled her bike out of the Greens' garage at about eight-twenty. She had a totally dismal expression on her face, and it didn't change when she saw us. "Oh, hi," was all she came up with.

"Have any news you'd like to tell us?" Kate said.

"Like what?" Stephanie asked warily.

"Like maybe you're having a family milestone this weekend?" I was cross, and tired of beating around the bush.

"I don't want to talk about it," was Stephanie's answer. She climbed on her bike and started pedaling determinedly up Pine.

"You like Mr. Kessler, don't you? You liked him at Lost Valley Ranch," I pointed out when we caught up with her. "We all did."

"And he and Nana look so happy together," Patti said. "You want them to be happy, don't you?" Those were practically the exact words that Stephanie had said to Patti about Uncle Nick and Ms. Chipley.

"Nana's going to have *him* to take care of now!"

75

Stephanie suddenly wailed. "I'm not going to matter anymore!"

"She's not going to care about you any less," Kate said. "In fact, she'll care about you more. Love multiplies. Isn't that what you told Patti not five days ago?"

"That's right, Stephanie." Patti smiled anxiously.

"I was trying to cheer Patti up! Who could believe anything they read in a magazine that said vests would be *out* this year?!" Stephanie said, sunk in gloom. "The truth is, everything's going to change, everything! Nana'll give up her apartment in the city and move to Maine with that man, and I'll *never* see her again!"

Patti's smile had disappeared. Her face fell, and by the time we got to school, I was feeling pretty grim myself.

And Stephanie didn't change her tune, even though Nana took her to Just Juniors to buy two new outfits that afternoon. Then Patti spent most of Thursday looking at pictures of herself and Uncle Nick together over the years, and sighing a lot. She actually brought a pile of them to school!

"Weddings seem to belong more under 'disasters' than 'milestones,' " Kate said to me in private.

"Yeah, I never knew they were so depressing," I agreed.

We managed to struggle through the rest of the week somehow. The sleepover would be at Patti's that Friday night. And she asked us if we could get to her house early, around six o'clock.

"Ms. Chipley" — we'd lost "Tara" and we were back to "Ms. Chipley" — "wants us to have dinner with her at her apartment," Patti told us. "She'll pick us up at my house at six. I guess she wants to talk about . . . ," her voice fell to a whisper, "the wedding."

"Don't even say that word," Stephanie muttered.

"She'd like it if you'd bring the bridesmaid's dress," Patti told Stephanie. "And she asked if you'd bring the video camera, Kate."

"What for?" Kate asked.

Patti shrugged. "Maybe to film one of us in the dress, to show to Amanda Tilton, her maid of honor."

"Oh, OK," Kate said.

So that evening, the four of us crammed into

Ms. Chipley's little blue car, along with the long, flat box with the dusty-pink bridesmaid's dress in it, and the camera. We drove to her apartment on Summit Boulevard, not far from Munn's Pond and the Wildlife Refuge.

Kate, Stephanie, and I had never been there before. It was nice, two bedrooms and a small kitchen on the second floor of a big, old house, and Ms. Chipley had decorated it really nicely, too, in bright, sunny colors — yellow and peach.

"She has *four hundred* dark-green towels already!" Kate whispered to me when we checked out the bathroom.

"She was just trying to think of something we could give her for a wedding present that wouldn't cost too much," I whispered back. I was starting to like Ms. Chipley more and more.

Actually, she seemed a lot livelier than she had the last time we'd seen her, at Patti's house. Sort of excited, and happy. She poured us all Cokes, and we sat down on the couch. I was just beginning to wonder where dinner was — I hadn't spotted any food in the kitchen, and I was starving — when the doorbell rang.

The pizza man? I swallowed in anticipation. But Ms. Chipley asked, "Kate, could you please get your camera ready?"

Kate nodded uncertainly and picked up the video camera. Maybe it was Amanda Tilton at the door?

Then Ms. Chipley said, "Patti, would you mind opening the door?"

So Patti stood up, walked to the door, and turned the knob. "Uncle Nick!" she screamed.

He grabbed Patti and swung her around a few times, grinning at Ms. Chipley and beaming at the rest of us. And Kate filmed it all.

"What are you doing here?!" Patti said, once Uncle Nick had put her down and she'd gotten her breath back.

"Yeah! Why aren't you in Europe?" Stephanie snapped out of her gloom long enough to ask.

"I had an interview for a very interesting job in the city," Uncle Nick answered.

"Did you get it?" Patti shrieked.

"Of course I did!" Uncle Nick said, swinging her around again.

"So you'll be living in the United States now?"

I asked, just to make sure I had it straight.

"I'll be here in a month," Uncle Nick said. "I'll have to go back to Europe first and finish what I was working on there, and pack up, of course."

We all nodded.

"But I'd hate to leave Tara again," he said in a lower voice. He walked over to Ms. Chipley and put his arm around her. He kissed the tip of her nose, just like Kevin DeSpain kisses Marcy Monroe on *Made for Each Other*, on Tuesday nights. Then Uncle Nick smiled the widest smile I've ever seen. "So we came up with a great idea," he said. "We're going to elope!"

"Elope!" the four of us repeated dumbly.

"You mean, like crawling out the window . . . ," Kate began from behind her video camera.

"Onto a ladder!" Uncle Nick finished for her. "I've got a ladder waiting outside, as a matter of fact." It sounded a little like one of Stephanie's plans, before she got bummed out about Nana and Mr. Kessler!

"And we'd like you to film the whole thing, Kate," Ms. Chipley added, looking up at Uncle Nick. "That way, everyone who's been planning a big wedding for us, like Patti's mom and my mom and

Amanda, can watch the video and not feel so left out." So Ms. Chipley hadn't wanted a huge ceremony *at all*.

"We thought Patti could wear the bridesmaid's dress, too, so she wouldn't miss out on being a bridesmaid," Ms. Chipley went on.

"We've even got rice for everybody to throw," Uncle Nick said, stepping into the kitchen and coming out with a big, brand-new box of it.

"Nick's arranged everything," Ms. Chipley said, her eyes shining. "We'll drive to Judge Frayne's house as soon as we drop you off."

Judge Frayne was going to have a busy weekend, I was thinking.

"He'll marry us, we'll spend a night in the city, and we'll catch a plane back to France tomorrow," Uncle Nick went on. "You girls will have to keep this a secret until then. But don't worry. We'll call everybody from the airport tomorrow evening, to let them know."

"And we'll be back before you've even noticed we're gone," Ms. Chipley said, giving Patti a hug. "And as soon as we find an apartment in the city, the four of you will be the first to visit us!"

"Great," Patti said, and she grinned.

I don't know how Stephanie felt about it, but I was beginning to think the article in *Teen Topics* was absolutely right. There was enough love in that room to light up all of Riverhurst. Patti was in heaven!

Marriage wasn't suddenly turning Uncle Nick into the boring kind of grown-up, either. There actually *was* a ladder outside Ms. Chipley's bedroom window, and she was going to use it to climb down to the ground!

Patti put on the bridesmaid's dress — she looked *great* in it! Then we all waited at the bottom of the ladder to throw rice. Kate filmed up to the moment that Ms. Chipley and Uncle Nick jumped into the blue car and sped away.

They had to turn around and come back for us, of course. And we all sang "Here Comes the Bride" as they drove us back to the Jenkinses'. Then they dropped us off at the end of Patti's street, so no one would see them.

As Patti practically *danced* up Mill Road toward her house, Kate patted the video camera and said, "This is the 'milestone' of the *century!*"

And even Stephanie mumbled, "Maybe *Teen Topics* was right after all. Maybe vests *are* out this year. . . ."

Chapter
9

I guess anything would seem a little tame after *that,* but Nana and Mr. Kessler's wedding was pretty terrific, too. It was small, just Stephanie's parents, and Emma and Jeremy in their fanciest baby clothes, and Mr. Kessler's brother, who'd flown in from Florida. And at the last minute, Stephanie decided to wear the dusty-pink bridesmaid's dress. She looked fabulous in it, too — even though it was almost full-length on her, and it only came to just below Patti's knees! I was almost a little jealous that Kate and I hadn't come up with weddings of our own to wear it to!

We stood in a circle in Judge Frayne's living room, with Nana and Mr. Kessler in the middle.

They'd written some of their own words for the ceremony, like how they'd always care for each other, no matter what, and how lucky they were to have so many special people in their lives. I gave Stephanie a good, sharp poke with my elbow, just in case she wasn't paying close enough attention.

Then we all drove back to the Greens' house, and I'd never seen so much fabulous food! It definitely made up for missing out on Uncle Nick and Ms. Chipley's wedding banquet. There was yummy pasta salad, little cherry tomatoes stuffed with cheese, shish kebabs, salmon spread shaped like a real fish — excellent! *And* there was a three-story wedding cake, white on the outside, chocolate on the inside, all of it from the Gilded Lobster, the most expensive restaurant in Riverhurst. There was more than enough to satisfy even my appetite!

Uncle Nick and Ms. Chipley weren't the only ones with surprises, either, because when Mr. Kessler's brother said to Nana, "So I guess you'll be giving up your apartment in the city," Nana hugged Stephanie close and said, "And leave my grandchildren? I couldn't do that!"

Stephanie looked up at her. "No?" she said.

"Absolutely not!" Mr. Kessler answered. "We'll live in the city in the cold weather, and Maine in the warm weather. It'll be the best of both worlds!"

Stephanie looked ecstatic. "Aren't weddings the best?" she whispered to Kate and Patti and me.

"You girls are going to love Maine!" Mr. Kessler added, looking at the four of us. "There's swimming, sailing, and the people next door have three boys in their family, with twins about your age . . ."

I couldn't wait.

That afternoon, Mr. and Mrs. Kessler left for San Francisco on their honeymoon. Once we'd changed out of our wedding duds and back into jeans, Kate, Stephanie, Patti, and I met in front of my house. We were just about to bike to the mall to look at towels again, when a brown car came driving slowly up Pine Street. It stopped briefly in front of every other house.

"Reading the numbers on the doors," Kate murmured.

"Maybe we can help," said Patti, nodding hello as the car pulled up next to us.

"Excuse me," the woman inside said, leaning

out the window. "Can you tell me where number eighteen is?"

I almost fainted! It was *Annabelle Dodson Brant,* in the flesh! Our letter had worked!

Her hair was shorter. In the 1942 yearbook, she'd had one of those long, sleek hairstyles. She wasn't wearing dark-red lipstick like she did back then, either. But otherwise, nothing had changed very much. There was a little gray in her hair and her face was a bit plumper, but I recognized her immediately, and so did everybody else!

"Mr. Winkler's house? It's that white one, with the beige shutters, across the street," Kate said smoothly.

"Thank you," Annabelle said, giving us a nice smile.

As she drove past the Martins', and the Baileys', and turned into Mr. Winkler's driveway, Kate, Stephanie, Patti, and I joined hands and jumped up and down — silently, of course. We'd done it! Our troubles with the Scourge of Pine Street were over!

We sat down on the curb and watched as Annabelle D. Brant got out of her car and knocked on Mr. Winkler's front door. The door opened, and she stepped inside.

"We might as well go," Kate said. "This could take all afternoon."

But we'd barely gotten to our feet when Mr. Winkler's door flew open. Annabelle marched out with a scowl on her face.

"Harvey Winkler," we heard her say, "you haven't changed a bit. You're still a — a stubborn grouch!"

"And you're still as flighty as ever!" Mr. Winkler fumed. "The idea that I would send you a letter. It's totally ridiculous!"

And with that Mr. Winkler slammed the door, while Annabelle marched down the steps, got into her car, and started the engine.

"You know how the article in *Teen Topics* said that if you love somebody, the love multiplies?" I murmured as the brown car shot out of Mr. Winkler's driveway. "I wonder if the opposite is true, too. . . ."

"If it is, I'm glad we have two apartments to stay in in the city," Patti said, "because we're going to need them!"

"What about *the personals?*" Stephanie wondered, her mind racing toward a new plan. "We could put an ad in the paper for Mr. Winkler: 'Distinguished older man, interested in the theater, gardening . . . ,' " until Kate gave her a shove and we all started to giggle.

Things were back to normal — it was Sleepover Friends, forever!

#26 The New Kate

We pulled our bikes over to the shoulder of the road and waited until Bitsy screeched to a stop beside us. She took a deep breath. Then she blurted out one long stream of words in a high, quavery voice: "I-know-you-guys-have-a-sleepover-together-every-Friday-and-you-probably-won't-want-to-do-this-but-I-wondered-if-you'd-like-to-come-to-my-house-I'd-*love*-to-have-you — " Then Bitsy ran out of air, or courage, or both, so she stopped and blinked at us nervously.

"Well, since tomorrow was supposed to be Kate's night . . ." I began.

"And Kate isn't going to be here . . ." Patti went on.

"We'd love to come!" Stephanie finished.